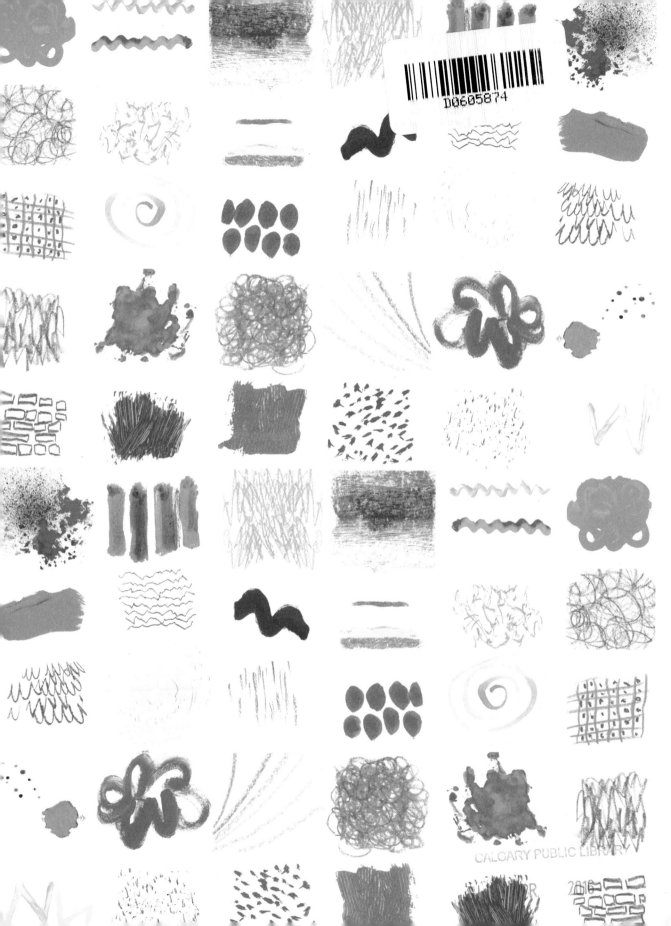

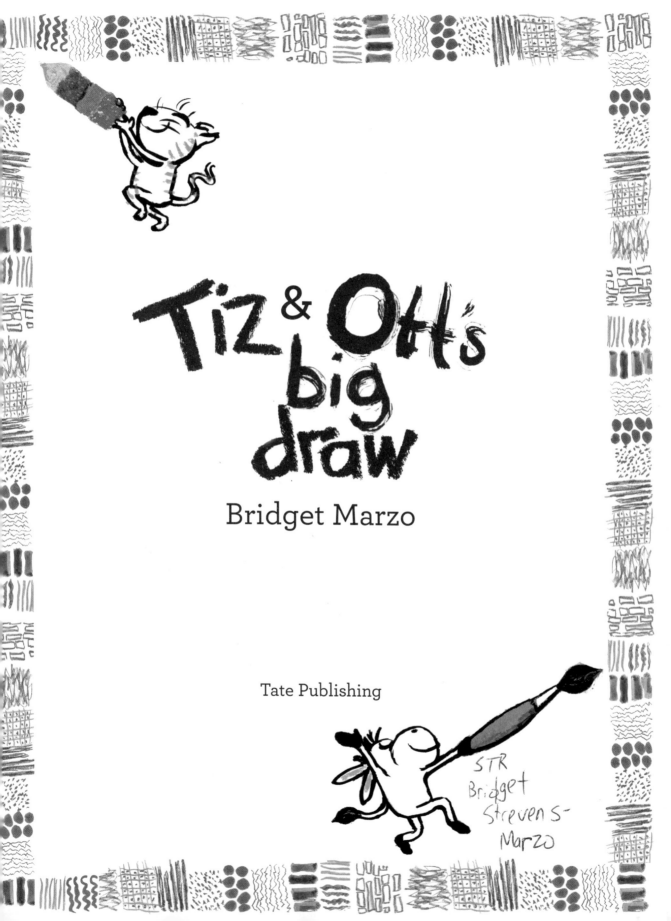

Tiz & Ott's big draw

Bridget Marzo

Tate Publishing

STR
Bridget
Strevens-
Marzo

Tiz was hard at work.

Ott was dabbling.

When the house was done ...

... Tiz started on the garden.

I'll do the seeds!
said Tiz.
You do the sun!

Ott yawned.
SPLODGE

The sun's too hot, Ott!
said Tiz.
Let's make some shade.

EASY! said Ott.

He could paint a cloud
with his eyes closed.

... and let's make it rain!
said Tiz.

Ott?

Where are you?

Oh!
There you are, Ott.
said Tiz.

ZZZZZ, went Ott.

Your brush
is just what I need ...

... *for my big idea.*

ZIG-
ZAG
C

Ott woke up
in a lightning flash.
Where's my brush?

They whipped up a storm until ...

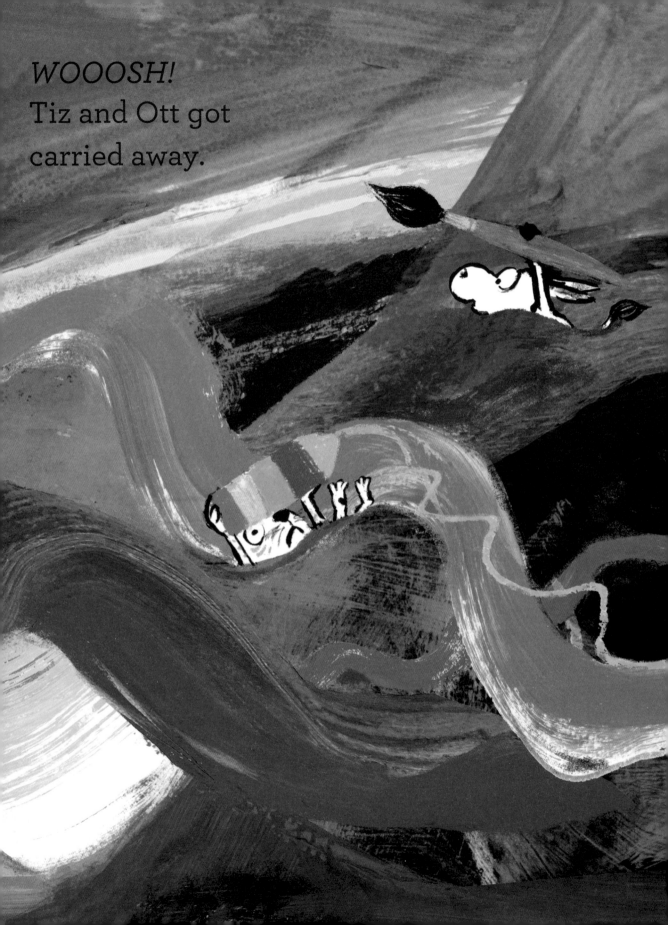

WOOOSH!
Tiz and Ott got
carried away.

SPLAT! went Ott into the sand.

SCRIBBLE THUMP!
went Tiz into a hole.

Tiz and Ott were stuck.
All Ott could do was
wave his brush until
flip flap
out flew a bird.

SCRITCH SCRATCH

Rung by rung,
Tiz made
her way
out of the hole.

Up went Tiz ...
so high....

TOO HIGH!

What to do?

Tiz drew and drew
and a bird showed
her a way ...

Down
down
down
to dig Ott out!

Weeeeeee!

Yippee!

Tiz and Ott
brushed
and doodled,
scrawled
and splattered,
scribbled
and scumbled,

And together,
they made their own way...

home.

How to draw me, Tiz

eyes

mouth

eyebrows   whiskers   tail

How to paint me, Ott

eyes

mouth

tail

How to make **a great, big mess!**

How Tiz and Ott make their marks

splatter

brushy

scrunchy

dollop

scrawl

wavy

shade

splodge

pitter patter

drip

blot

waggle

slant

zig zag

dots

dashes

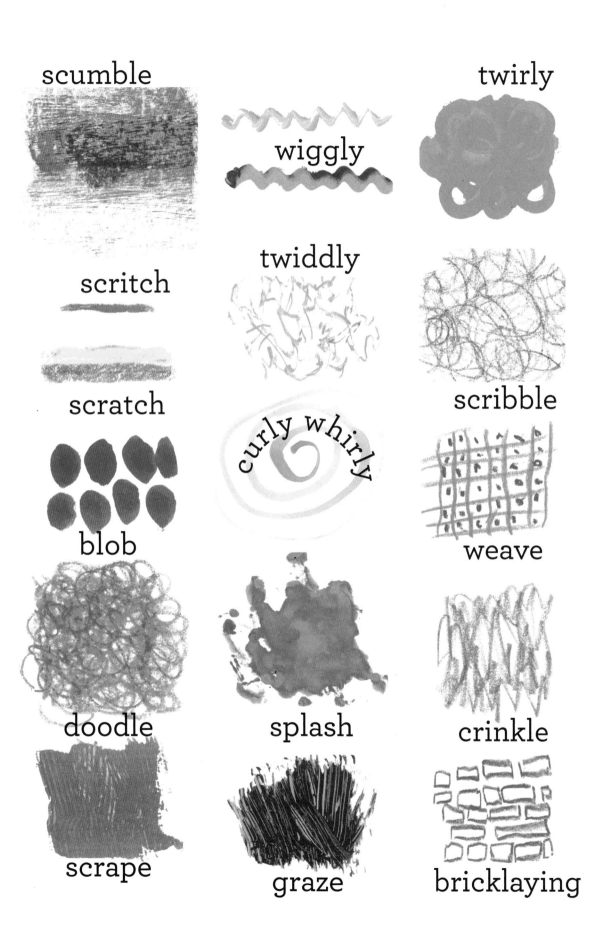

scumble

twirly

wiggly

scritch

twiddly

scratch

scribble

blob

curly whirly

weave

doodle

splash

crinkle

scrape

graze

bricklaying

First published 2015 by order of the Tate Trustees
by Tate Publishing, a division of Tate Enterprises Ltd,
Millbank, London SW1P 4RG
www.tate.org.uk/publishing

A catalogue record for this book is available from
the British Library
ISBN 978 1 84976 310 3

Distributed in the United States and Canada by
ABRAMS, New York
Library of Congress Control Number applied for

Colour reproduction by DL Imaging London
Printed in China by Toppan Leefung Printing Ltd

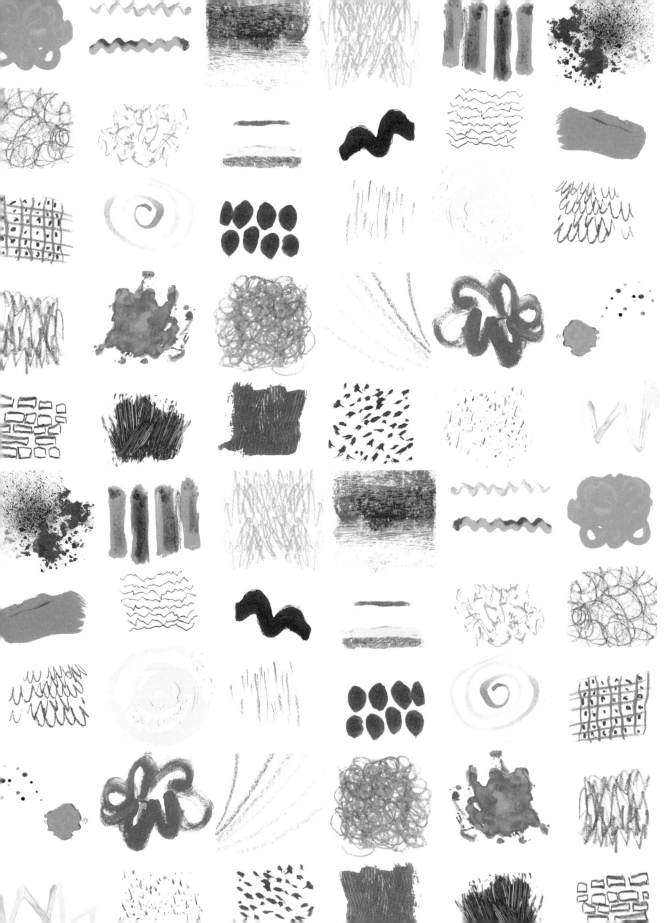